568.1 Parish, Peggy.
PAR
Dinosaur time.

$13.89   33197000016373

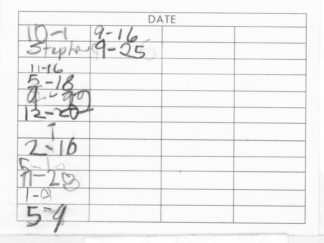

DATE			
10-1	9-16		
Stephen	9-25		
11-16			
5-18			
9-30			
12-20			
2-16			
5-28			
1-8			
5-9			

An I Can Read Book®

DINOSAUR TIME

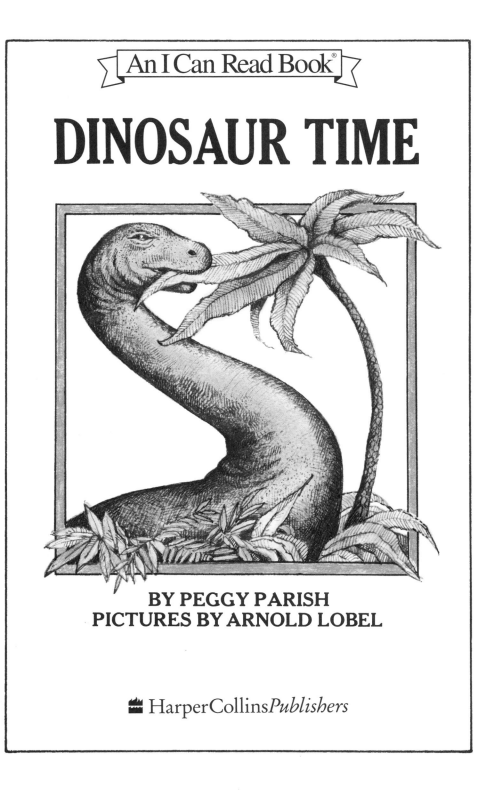

BY PEGGY PARISH
PICTURES BY ARNOLD LOBEL

HarperCollins*Publishers*

for Betsy and Rob Reid—
with love

I Can Read Book is a registered trademark of HarperCollins Publishers.

DINOSAUR TIME
Text copyright © 1974 by Margaret Parish
Illustrations copyright © 1974 by Arnold Lobel
For information address HarperCollins
Children's Books, a division of HarperCollins Publishers, 10 East 53rd
Street, New York, NY 10022.

Library of Congress Catalog Card Number: 73-14331
ISBN 0-06-024653-7
ISBN 0-06-024654-5 (lib. bdg.)

The Dinosaurs

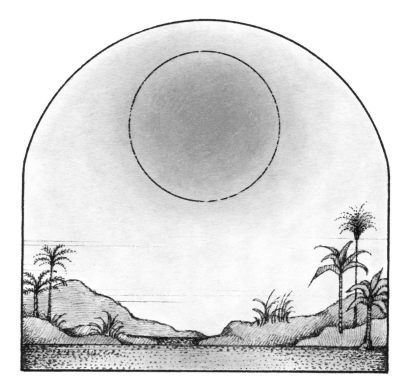

Long, long ago

the world was different.

More land was under water.

It was warm all the time.

And dinosaurs

were everywhere. . . .

6

There were big dinosaurs.

There were small ones.

There were fast dinosaurs,
and slow ones.

Some dinosaurs ate meat.

Some ate plants.

STEGOSAURUS

This is how you say it—

steg-uh-SAW-russ

This dinosaur

had plates on its back.

They were made of bone.

It had sharp points

on its tail.

It ate plants.

Its name is Stegosaurus.

DIPLODOCUS

This is how you say it—

dip-LAH-duh-cuss

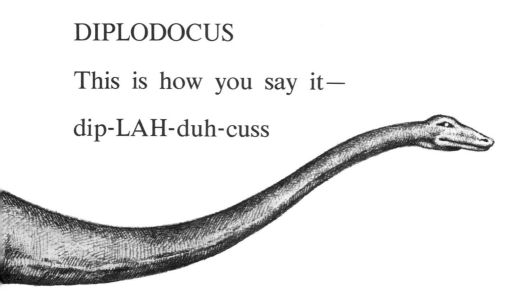

This dinosaur was long.

But most of it was neck and tail.

Its teeth were short and dull.

It ate plants.

Its name is Diplodocus.

ANKYLOSAURUS

This is how you say it—

ank-eye-loh-SAW-russ

This dinosaur

had a shell like a turtle.

Its tail was like a club.

Not many animals

could hurt it.

Its name is Ankylosaurus.

BRONTOSAURUS

This is how you say it—

bron-tuh-SAW-russ

This dinosaur

was a giant.

But its mouth was tiny.

It ate plants.

It ate, and ate, and ate

to fill up its big body.

Its name is Brontosaurus.

COMPSOGNATHUS

This is how you say it—

comp-sog-NAYTH-uss

This dinosaur

was small.

It was as big as a cat.

But it could run fast.

It could catch other animals

and eat them.

Its name is Compsognathus.

TERATOSAURUS

This is how you say it—

tare-at-oh-SAW-russ

This dinosaur

walked on its back legs.

It had big claws,

and sharp teeth.

It ate meat.

Its name is Teratosaurus.

ANATOSAURUS

This is how you say it—

an-at-oh-SAW-russ

This dinosaur

is called a "duckbill."

It had a beak like a duck.

Its beak had no teeth.

But its mouth did.

There were hundreds

of teeth in it!

Sometimes a tooth broke.

But that did not matter.

It could grow a new one.

Its name is Anatosaurus.

ORNITHOMIMUS

This is how you say it—

or-nith-oh-MY-muss

This dinosaur had a beak, too.

But it had no teeth.

It ate small animals and insects.

Maybe it ate fruits

and dinosaur eggs, too.

But it had no teeth.

How did it eat?

A bird eats.

It has no teeth.

Maybe it ate

like a bird.

Its name is

Ornithomimus.

BRACHIOSAURUS

This is how you say it—

brack-ee-oh-SAW-russ

This dinosaur was fat.

It was too fat

to run from enemies.

That is why it stayed in the water.

It was safe there,

and food was close by.

It ate plants.

Its name is Brachiosaurus.

PENTACERATOPS

This is how you say it—

pen-tuh-SARE-ah-tops

This dinosaur had five horns.

They were all on its face.

Its name is Pentaceratops.

This name is just right.

It means "five-horns-on-the-face."

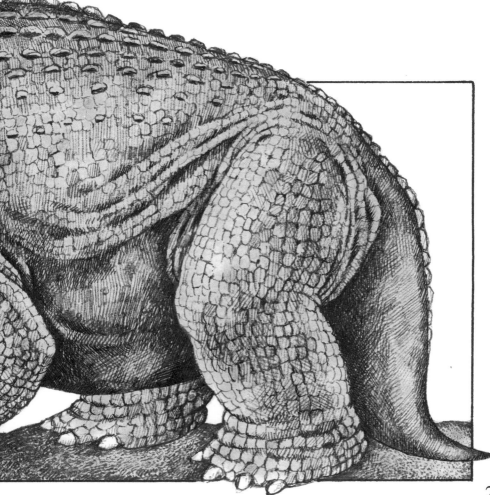

TYRANNOSAURUS

This is how you say it—

tih-ran-uh-SAW-russ

This dinosaur

was the biggest meat-eater.

Its jaws were huge.

Its teeth were six inches long.

It ate other dinosaurs.

Its name is Tyrannosaurus.

Dinosaurs lived everywhere

for a long time.

Then they died.

Nobody knows why.

But once it was their world.

It was dinosaur time.

Author's Note

We do not know much about dinosaurs. No one ever saw a dinosaur.

But people have found dinosaur
fossils, such as footprints, bones, and
teeth. Scientists study them, and can
tell how big the dinosaurs were, what
they ate, and other things about the
way they lived.

Scientists learn more each year.
But we may never know all about
dinosaurs.

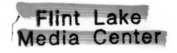